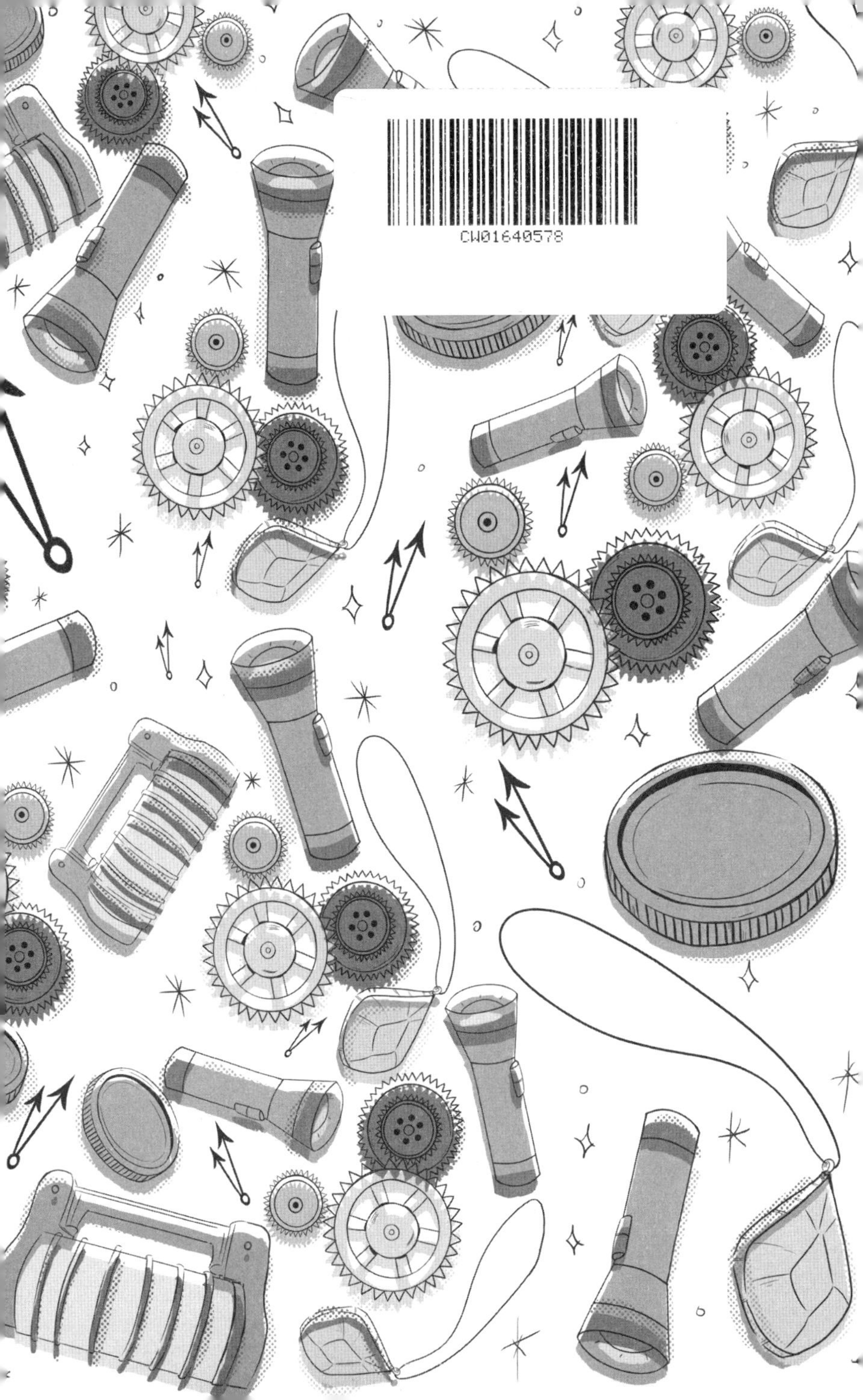

CW01640578

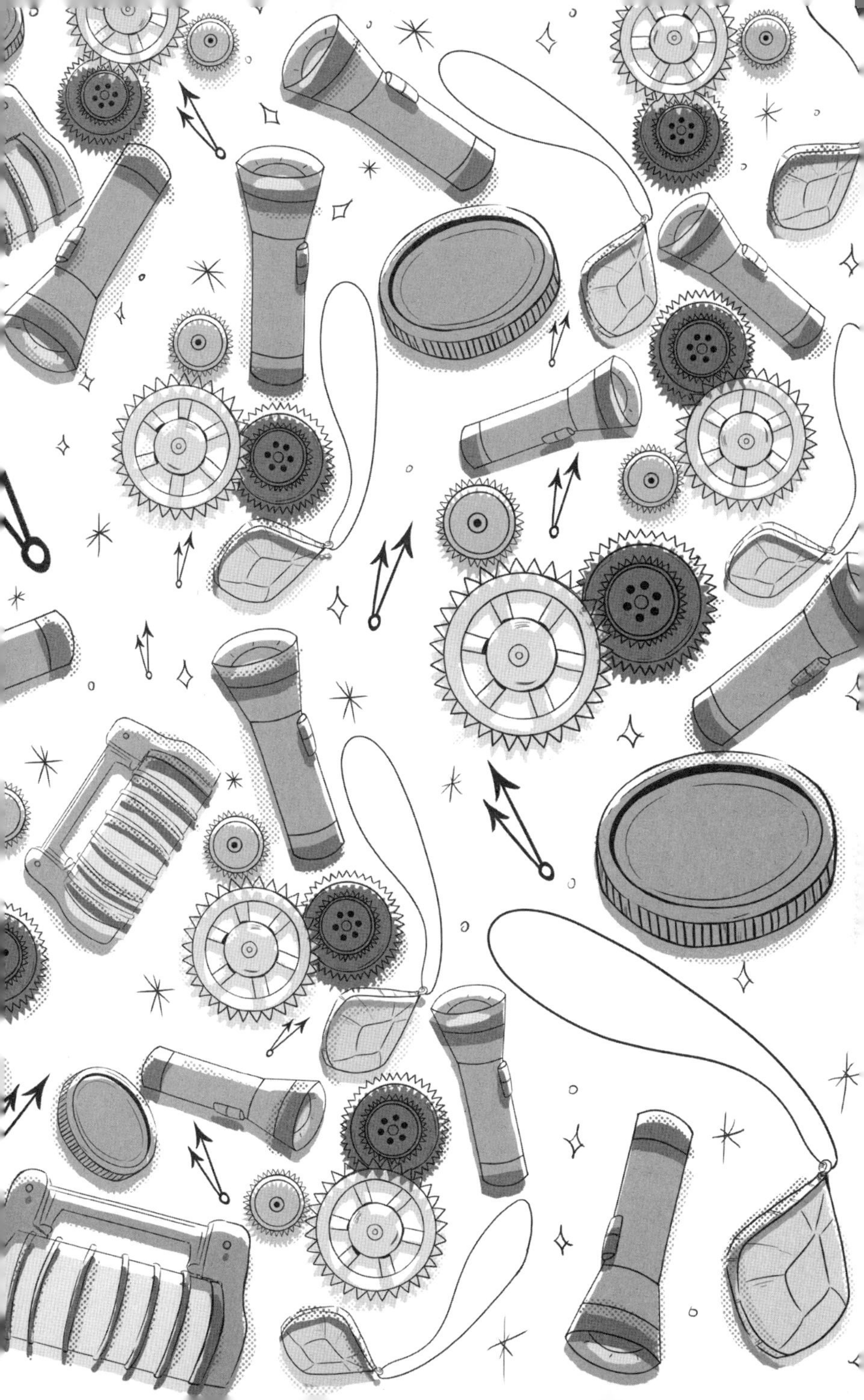

The Thirteenth Chime of Alcott Hall

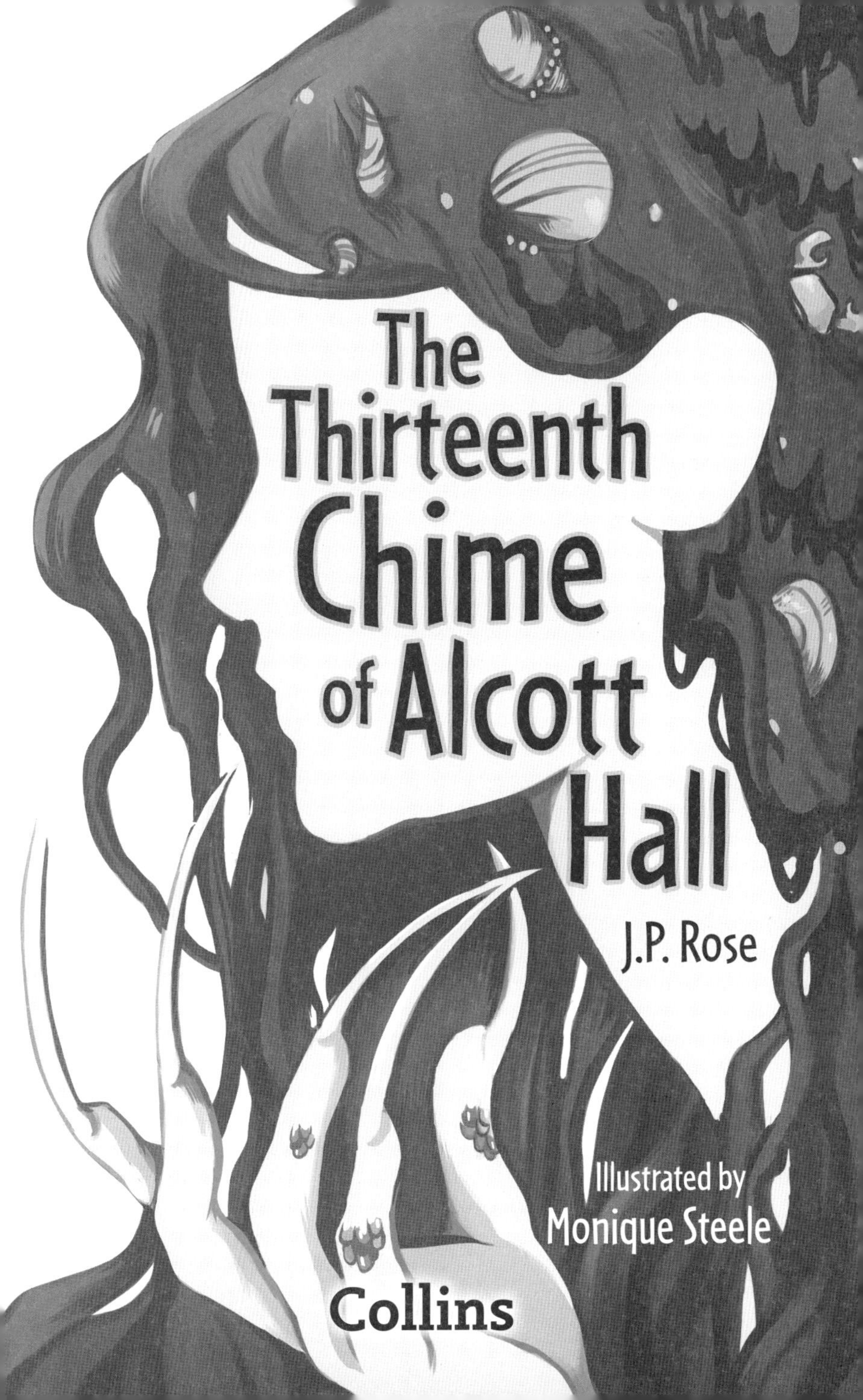
The Thirteenth Chime of Alcott Hall
J.P. Rose
Illustrated by
Monique Steele
Collins

Chapter 1

Lola Avery slumped in the back seat of her parent's old car as it clattered and chugged its way up the winding cliff road, grumbling at every turn. They'd been driving for hours, and Lola hoped the journey wouldn't take much longer. This morning, they'd got up very early, leaving behind the built-up area of Oxford, and now they were making their way through pretty little Cornish villages with houses painted in bright colours. She was surrounded by rolling hills, cliffs and golden beaches, and she'd spotted some surfers riding the waves, which looked a lot of fun.

A few minutes' drive from the tiny village of Cove Green, Lola suddenly sat up and pressed her forehead against the cool window. "Whoa," she whispered, as they drove through a large set of rusted iron gates. "Is this where we're staying?"

"It looks a fantastic place to spend the summer, doesn't it?" Mum said. She turned round in the front seat and gave Lola a beaming smile.

Lola's eyes widened as the huge, crumbling Victorian mansion covered in creeping ivy came into view. It had a large clock tower, and a weathered sign creaked in the breeze. She leant forward, squinting to read the faded letters on the sign: Alcott Hall.

"Are you *sure* we should stay here?" Lola glanced nervously at the manor house. It seemed to stare back at her.

Her dad looked at her in the rear-view mirror and chuckled. "Come on, Lo. Where's your sense of adventure? You know, when I was a kid growing up in Jamaica, I loved discovering new places during the holidays." He smiled. "It'll be fun, and you've got the whole of the summer holidays ahead to explore."

"But it seems … it seems – " Lola paused. "Well, it seems … *old*."

Dad roared with laughter. "That's what makes it so great, and besides, Gran needs our help to restore some of the furniture for the new owner before they move in. It'll be lovely for us all to spend some time together."

They pulled up to the big front door, and Lola stepped out of the car, stretching her legs. She walked along a small path and looked up at the mansion, which sat alone on the cliff, with the wild sea and crashing waves below.

She yawned but then snapped her mouth shut quickly. *Huh*? Did a curtain in one of the upper windows twitch? She gasped as she saw multiple faces pressed against the window, all staring down at her.

"Mum! *Mum!*"

Her mum pushed her long, blonde hair behind her ears and looked over. "Everything all right?"

Lola pointed to the window but when she did

there was no one there. She rubbed her eyes. "I thought I saw – " She shrugged and shook her head. "Nothing." She frowned. It must've been a reflection she'd seen, although that thought didn't stop Lola hurrying back over to where her mum and dad were standing.

Before she could think about it any longer, the front door flew open. Out bounded an enormous grey Great Dane, with large velvety ears, followed by a whirlwind of colourful scarves and jangling bracelets. "You made it!" Gran gave Lola a wide smile, and her grey Afro locks moved as she waved. Her eyes sparkled behind her round, red glasses.

"Down, Donkey! Down!" Gran called, as the enormous dog bounded up to Lola, nearly knocking her off her feet. "Sorry, Lola, I think he forgets he's not a lapdog."

Lola steadied herself, patted Donkey's head and grinned. "Hi, Gran."

"So how about a nice cup of tea and some supper? Then I can show you round," Gran suggested. She held onto her scarves to stop them blowing away.

"That would be lovely." Lola's mum nodded eagerly, and her blue eyes sparkled warmly. "Thank you."

As they followed Gran into Alcott Hall, it began to rain, and Lola cast one more glance up at the window. For some reason, she couldn't stop a shiver shooting down her spine.

Chapter 2

With supper over, Lola followed her parents and Gran along the long corridors of Alcott Hall. It was raining hard now, and lightning cracked through the night sky.

"There are over 20 bedrooms and over ten bathrooms in Alcott Hall," Gran laughed. "It's easy to get lost; even Donkey gets lost sometimes."

Lola gazed through the open doors at the dusty rooms. A lot of the furniture was covered with dusty sheets, which made strange shapes in the dim light. It looked like people or monsters were hiding under there, waiting silently.

The lights suddenly flicked off and Lola shrieked.

"Oh, don't worry, this always happens, especially when there's a storm," Gran laughed. They were standing in a corridor, and a moment later, a beam of torchlight shone at Lola.

Gran stood holding a torch. "I always carry one, just in case," she said, cheerfully. "Hopefully the electricity will come back on soon … Come on, I'll show you where your rooms are."

Lola made sure she stayed close to her dad as they went back into the large hallway and up the grand flight of stairs. Gran stopped at a thick, wooden door with a big, brass doorknob. She opened it and shone the torch round.

"This one's your room, Lola. It was very dusty, but it's had a good clean now and fresh bedsheets. A big team came in from London and cleaned most of the place. There are still some rooms to do, but it took over ten people, and a whole week. Though it's not surprising." Gran laughed. "It hasn't been touched for a very long time. This room's lovely because the windows look out right across to the sea."

Lola didn't think there was anything lovely about it. The rain was pelting against the window and there was a large four-poster bed, and a huge stone fireplace. As Gran shone the torch around, Lola saw a painting of a stern old woman, much older than Gran. She wore a long, dark dress with puffy sleeves and lots of buttons. A high collar wrapped around her neck. On her head was a large, white bonnet with ribbons.

“This is great, isn’t it?” Mum said, as she walked into the room. “It’s huge.”

Just then the lights came on in the landing and Lola let out a sigh of relief. Gran switched on the bedroom light and immediately Lola felt better.

“I think you’ll sleep very well in here,” Gran smiled.

There was a loud creak followed by a rumble of thunder and Lola jumped.

“That’s just the old beams in the roof.” Gran looked up towards the ceiling. “Nothing to worry about.”

Lola wasn’t so sure. “Can Donkey stay with me tonight?”

Dad grinned and ruffled Lola’s crown of brown curls. “I’m sure Gran wouldn’t mind.”

“I think he’d like that.” Gran nodded. She called over her shoulder, “*Donkey!*”

A few seconds later, Donkey came bounding

in, his long ears flapping. Lola bent down and hugged him and in return, he gave her a great big lick. She giggled with delight, but her smile soon faded as she looked at the painting again. The old woman's eyes seemed to follow her.

Chapter 3

Lola's eyes snapped open in the darkness, her heart racing. She wasn't quite sure what had woken her up. She couldn't hear anything apart from the distant thunder as she lay in the enormous four-poster bed, feeling tiny in the huge, unfamiliar room. Donkey lay at the foot of her bed whilst faint moonlight filtered through the heavy curtains, casting eerie shadows across the antique furniture.

Needing a drink of water, Lola swung her legs out of bed and grabbed her dressing gown before opening the door. She crept along the landing which was bathed in a strange glow from an old flickering wall light.

Walking down the grand stairs, the deep

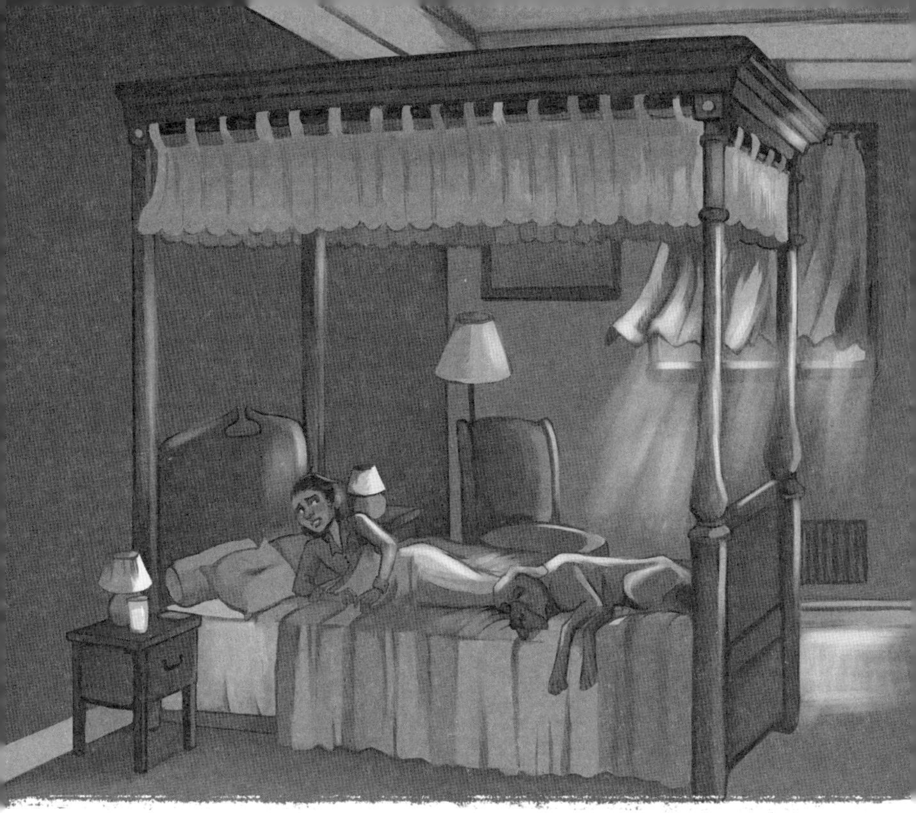

booming clock tower's bell started to chime … Lola counted silently: one … two … three … *That was strange*. The chimes had continued past twelve. Thirteen. The clock had just struck *thirteen times*. She frowned. Maybe she'd miscounted, but she was *sure* there'd been thirteen strikes of the clock tower's bell.

Then she froze.

In front of her, in the large entrance hall, a

roaring fire crackled in the massive fireplace. It hadn't been lit when she went to bed. Standing in front of it, silhouetted against the flames, was a woman. Her blue satin dress was long and flowing, reaching the floor. It had a tight waist and full skirt. Like the old woman's dress in the painting in her room, the sleeves were puffy at the shoulders; her hair was piled up high on her head.

Suddenly, the woman turned to stare at Lola. Her face was thin and as white as fresh snow. Her lips were blue and cracked, pressed into a tight line. She didn't blink as she kept her icy gaze fixed on Lola.

Lola held her breath. The woman began to move towards her! Shaking, Lola squeezed her eyes shut, feeling a cold chill run through her. Then, Lola felt something brush her cheek, and her eyes snapped open, but when she looked, the hallway was empty. The fire was out, cold and untouched, and Lola was alone in the darkness.

Chapter 4

"Good morning, Lola." Lola's dad smiled cheerfully as he sat at the kitchen table. "How did you sleep?"

"I hope Dad's snoring didn't wake you up," Mum added, laughing. "It was almost as loud as the thunder."

Dad chuckled and took a sip of coffee. The bright morning sunshine shone through the windows.

Lola glanced around the shiny new kitchen which Gran had said the builders only finished a week ago. It was bright and modern, and Lola had to admit the house didn't look as scary as it had last night. But she still had an uneasy feeling.

"Come and have some breakfast whilst there's still some left," Gran said. "Your dad has nearly finished all the dumplings."

Gran was wearing a bright red dress with a yellow belt, which was so different to the woman Lola had seen in the hallway.

Dad patted his tummy. "I need all the food I can get this morning if I'm going to be helping move furniture down from the attic for you."

Gran scooped another large spoon of ackee from the blue bowl on the table and added it to Dad's plate.

Lola sat down quietly. She looked at the table full of food: fried dumplings, ackee and plantain. Every time they stayed with Gran, she always cooked something tasty, but this wasn't Gran's house and right now Lola didn't feel like eating.

"Is everything all right, Lola?" Mum sounded concerned.

"I didn't sleep very well," Lola admitted.

Gran frowned. "Oh dear, did the storm keep you awake?"

Lola shook her head as Donkey walked into the room; he was after some of Gran's delicious food. "No, it was – " She took a deep breath. "Well, I couldn't sleep because I saw someone standing in the hall."

"What?" Dad sat up in his chair. He wiped some dumpling crumbs from his goatee with a tissue. "Who?"

Lola shrugged. "I don't know. But when I came downstairs, she was standing in front of the roaring fire, and she was dressed in old-fashioned clothes." Her words rushed out. She didn't want to think about the woman. And last night, she hadn't even bothered to get the water she'd gone downstairs for. Instead she'd rushed back upstairs and spent the rest of the night with the light on cuddled up with Donkey.

Lola glanced at Mum, Dad and Gran.

The grown-ups looked back at her seriously, then a large smile crossed Dad's face and he burst out laughing. "You and your imagination, Lo," he said, not unkindly.

"I'm not imagining it. I saw her. I know I did, I know." Lola turned to Gran. "She was just standing there in front of the fire but then she suddenly disappeared, and then the fire went out."

"It sounds to me like you were dreaming, Lola," Gran said.

"I wasn't. She was *definitely* there. Why won't you believe me?"

"Come with me." Gran held out her hand for Lola to take.

They walked through to the hallway where the grand stone fireplace was. "I want to show you something." Gran pointed. "Look, there can't have been a fire. Just before you came, I cleaned all the dust out. There probably hasn't been a fire there since the previous owners lived here."

Lola stared at the empty fireplace and the stone hearth. Gran was right. It was spotless. There was no sign of anything having been there, not even dust, but that didn't make sense. Could she really have been dreaming? She was so *sure* that she'd woken up and walked down the stairs to get a drink and seen the woman standing there. But then … she sighed. Maybe Gran was right.

"Don't worry. Sometimes when I'm in strange places, on the first night I have all sorts of dreams," Gran said, giving Lola a hug. "Why don't you have some breakfast, then you can explore the beach. It's going to be a lovely day today."

Lola nodded and began to make her way back to the kitchen, but as she did, she noticed the painting above the fireplace. It was of a family. One child, a boy, had on knee-length trousers and a smart jacket to match. The girl wore a frilly dress with a big bow in her hair. The man wore a dark navy suit with a high collar, and he had a pocket watch chain. Then Lola gasped. The woman in the

painting looked *exactly* like the one she'd seen last night in the hallway. None of them looked happy.

"Who are they?" Lola said quietly.

Gran looked at the painting. "Oh, that's the Alcott family. Captain Alfred Alcott and his wife, Lady Florence Alcott, and their children. If I remember the story rightly, they were called Bertha and Henry."

"Why is their painting here?" Lola asked.

"Captain Alcott and his wife were the original owners of Alcott Hall, and the new owner thought it would be nice to have the painting here. It's been restored and rehung."

Lola thought about it for a moment. "Why would they want to restore it?"

Gran smiled. "It's a snapshot into the past, and a way of keeping a record of history … especially as this is probably one of the last paintings of the Alcott family. It's a strange story really," Gran said, seriously.

"Why, what happened?" Lola asked.

"Well, when I was buying some bread in the village, the baker told me all about Alcott Hall; that's how I know the names of the Alcott family. It seems that one night in August 1875, the whole family disappeared. When the maids got up in the morning, the fire was still glowing, and the oil lamps were still burning. There was even a half-eaten bowl of soup in the dining room. No one knows what happened, no one heard anything, but no one saw any of them again."

Chapter 5

The sun was already high in the sky as Lola walked with Donkey along the beach. She'd taken her shoes off and she was enjoying feeling the warm sand between her toes. She was also pleased to be away from Alcott Hall. As grand and large as the place was, Lola thought there was something creepy about it. From where she was standing, she could see it looming on the top of the isolated cliff, looking dark and mean.

"Come on, Donkey, let's go this way." Lola put her shoes back on and wandered along to where the beach was pebbly; the waves crashed over them, making them look shiny and polished.

"*Hello!*"

Lola heard a voice behind her. She turned round and saw two kids sitting on a large rock. They both looked the same age as her and they waved. Lola waved back, and walked over to them.

The boy, who had short red hair and lots of freckles, looked at Lola through his blue-rimmed glasses. "Are you here on holiday?"

Lola nodded. "Yes, are you?"

He shook his head. "No, I live here. Well, I live in the village of Cove Green."

"I'm here on holiday," the girl smiled. She had a mass of long mousy blonde hair woven into loose plaits. There were red and yellow plastic beads threaded through them. She wore a flowing T-shirt and trousers with coloured beads. "I'm staying at the campsite on the other side of the village. My parents have gone to check out the market." She pulled a face. "I didn't want to go; they take ages looking around, but they never end up buying anything," she said. "I'm Poppy, by the way." She nudged the boy.

"Oh yeah, I'm Archie." He smiled broadly at Lola.

"I'm Lola," she smiled back. "How long have you two known each other?"

"Only for two weeks." Poppy shrugged. "We met at the village café when Mum and I were having breakfast. We've been hanging out ever since. Where are you staying?"

Lola pointed to the cliffs. "I'm staying at Alcott Hall for the summer with my parents and my gran."

Archie raised his eyebrows and pushed his glasses up his nose. "*Alcott Hall!* You're brave." He threw a pebble into one of the breaking waves, and Donkey immediately chased after it.

Lola frowned. "Brave?"

Archie nodded. "Don't you know? The place is *haunted*."

"Haunted!" Poppy exclaimed. "Really?"

"Yep, everyone around here knows about that place. No one's lived there since the Alcott family disappeared."

"But that was – " Lola tried to work out the maths and halfway through gave up. "Well, *ages ago*." Gran had said no one had stayed there for a long time, but she didn't realise the Alcotts were actually the last people to live there.

Archie became very animated. "The rest of the Alcott family had gone to live in the United States, so it's been empty since Victorian times. My dad says nothing's been changed since the night they disappeared."

Lola swallowed hard. "Are you sure?"

Archie nodded. "Nothing, not even the bedsheets," he whispered dramatically.

"No way!" Poppy stared at Lola.

Lola looked at Archie. She certainly didn't like the idea of sleeping in the bed if that was true, but then she remembered. "Well, the bed might be Victorian, but Gran said she'd put fresh sheets on it … Do you know who's coming to live in it now? Gran's restoring furniture for the new owner."

"Dad says that it's a distant relative of the Alcotts. Dad doesn't believe it's haunted though, he just thinks that it's people's imagination because they've heard the stories of the house."

Lola thought Archie's dad sounded very much like her own.

"My uncle thinks it's haunted though," Archie continued. "He says he doesn't think the new people will stay long."

"Why?" Poppy was wide-eyed.

Archie looked around as if someone was watching them. "Anyone who's ever entered that house has always seen something strange."

"Like what?" Poppy said, sounding as nervous as Lola felt.

Archie looked at Lola and Poppy and took a deep breath. "Ghosts."

Chapter 6

"I think I saw a ghost last night," Lola said, as Archie slid off the rock and came to sit next to her on the sand. They watched Donkey dig a great big hole.

Poppy gasped and came to sit down next to Lola too. "Wow, I thought this holiday was going to be boring, but it's turning out to be more interesting than I thought." She got a bottle of water out of her purple rucksack.

"Where did you see it?" Archie asked.

"Last night in the hallway when I was coming down for a drink of water … Mum and Dad didn't believe me. Neither did Gran when I told them this morning."

Archie glanced at Lola, looking very serious.

His face was very red from the sun. "I believe you."

"So do I," Poppy agreed.

Lola smiled at her new friends. "There was something else. Last night when I was walking down the stairs, I – " She suddenly stopped.

"What?" Poppy asked.

Lola shook her head. "It's probably nothing."

"Tell us anyway," Archie said.

"Well, I thought I heard the chime of the clock tower bell strike thirteen times."

"You heard the thirteenth chime?" Archie seemed very excited by this.

Lola looked at Archie in surprise. "I thought I did, I was sure I did, but then I thought maybe I was imagining it."

"Mr Humphries always says strange things happen on the thirteenth chime."

"Who's Mr Humphries?" Poppy asked.

"He's an horologist," Archie told them.

Poppy looked at Lola, then she looked back at Archie. "An horologist, what's that?"

Archie grinned. "It's a person who makes or repairs clocks or watches."

"So, he's a clockmaker," Poppy laughed, teasing him.

"He's got a shop in the village," Archie said. "He knows all about the thirteenth chime. I could take you there, if you like. I'm sure he'd speak to you. Why don't you go and tell your parents where we're going, and then we can go and talk to him."

Lola thought about it. Part of her wasn't sure if she wanted to speak to Mr Humphries.

Everything about Alcott Hall seemed spooky and she wasn't at all certain that she wanted to know any more than she did already, *especially* as she had to stay there for the next six weeks. The other part of her wanted to know *all* the secrets of Alcott Hall.

Poppy stood up and put her rucksack on her back. "Well, I want to know about it. How can a clock strike thirteen times?"

Lola stood up as well and pulled out Donkey's lead from her pocket. She looked at Poppy and Archie. "I don't know, but you're right. How about we go and find out?"

Chapter 7

Mr Humphries' clock shop was in the middle of Cove Green. It was a pretty village with a large oak tree and brightly coloured flowers in the centre of the cobbled square. There was a post office, a bakery and a fishmonger, a café with wooden tables and chairs at the front, and a small grocer's shop on the corner with fruit and vegetables outside.

The window display of Mr Humphries' shop was a dusty assortment of watches, clocks and various clock parts. There was a large tabby cat curled up in the centre of the window, snuggled up next to a broken cuckoo clock.

"Come on, let's go and see what he's got to say about Alcott Hall," Archie said, and without waiting for a reply from Lola or Poppy, he opened the door.

The bell above it rang and Lola looked around the shop. Donkey stared at the cat who stared back looking unconcerned. Like the window display, the shop itself was very dusty. Large grandfather clocks veiled in cobwebs lined the walls. There were shelves of watches, watchstraps and clocks with only one hand.

The shop was also very noisy. Clocks ticked loudly, all at different times, and bells chimed randomly, whilst cuckoos called out from their clocks every few minutes.

"Mr Humphries?" Archie called out, shouting above the din. "MR HUMPHRIES!" This time he shouted much louder and, after a few moments, an old man, with a long white beard and a thick head of white messy hair to match, shuffled through from the back room. He wore a tweed suit with a knitted green cardigan over the top of it.

Mr Humphries' face lit up. "Hello, Archie. I didn't hear you in the back – next time you need to call out."

Archie smiled at Lola, who smiled back at him. She'd imagined that she'd spend most of the summer alone whilst Mum and Dad helped Gran. Now she'd made two new friends on the first day of the holidays, and they were investigating ghosts.

"What can I do for you today?" Mr Humphries said, as he threw the biscuit he'd partly eaten to Donkey, who caught it and wolfed it down. "Are you looking for a present for someone? They might like this." He picked up a broken watch out of a wooden box. "Or this?" Mr Humphries reached into another box and

showed Archie a small wooden cuckoo from one of the broken clocks.

Archie shook his head. “Not today, thank you, Mr Humphries. I wanted to introduce you to my new friends, Lola and Poppy. Lola’s staying at Alcott Hall.”

Mr Humphries stared at Lola, then slumped down in the wooden chair by the counter. “Oh, my dear.” His face paled. He lowered his voice and Lola leant in to hear what he was saying. “My advice to you is, go back to the hall, pack up your things and get out of there today."

Lola felt a sudden fear pass over her. "But I can't. Mum and Dad are helping Gran restore the furniture."

Mr Humphries looked quite ill now. He shook his head. "It's not safe for you to be there. Don't you know it's haunted? No one dares work there, let alone stay there. Someone put a notice up in the post office on behalf of the new owner. He was looking for a gardener and a cleaner, but no one round these parts is silly enough to enter Alcott Hall." He visibly shivered. "You poor girl."

Poppy gave Lola a sympathetic smile.

"Lola heard the thirteenth chime," Archie said, looking worried.

To make Lola feel even worse, Mr Humphries gasped and covered his mouth.

"I heard it last night when I got up to go and get a drink," Lola said shakily. "That's when I saw the woman. She was standing in front of the fire in the hallway, but then she disappeared, and the fire went out. This morning, there was no sign that a fire had ever been there." She frowned. "The woman I saw looked exactly the same as the woman in the painting above the fireplace. Gran says the picture is of the Alcotts."

Mr Humphries nodded. He stared at Lola, sombrely. "That'll be Mrs Alcott. She's been seen on many occasions ... Why don't you come through to the back, and I'll tell you all about the Alcott tragedy."

Chapter 8

After searching for the kettle under a mound of clocks and clock parts, Lola eventually found it hidden between an old grandfather clock and a pile of clock hands. She made Mr Humphries a cup of tea with several spoons of honey in it, whilst she and Poppy had apple juice and Archie had a glass of lemonade.

Mr Humphries took a loud sip of tea. "Like I say, no one has dared to stay at Alcott Hall since the Alcott family's disappearance."

"But does no one want to find out about what happened to them?" Lola asked.

Mr Humphries nodded. "I think folk have tried, but they soon get scared off by all the strange sightings."

Poppy leant forward and spoke quietly. "What strange sightings?"

"Are you sure you want to hear this?" Mr Humphries said.

Lola looked at Poppy and then at Archie, and slowly they all nodded at the same time.

"Well," Mr Humphries continued. "Instead of striking twelve, the clock at Alcott Hall always chimes thirteen times. Legend has it, the thirteenth chime only started happening when the Alcott family disappeared. And on the thirteenth chime, people have reported hearing screams and seeing ghostly figures walking through the corridors. People walking their dogs late at night have seen faces at the windows and lights flickering on and off, even though there was nobody living there. There have even been reports of the sound of music playing loudly. Then there's the doors banging and windows opening and closing on their own, and Mr Rogers from the bakery said that when his dog ran into the grounds, and he had to go and find him, he saw Mrs Alcott standing at the front door calling to him and waving him inside."

Lola gulped.

"That was the last time Mr Rogers ever went near the place as you can imagine." Mr Humphries took another gulp of his tea.

"I thought I saw people at the window when I arrived," Lola said, remembering the faces pressed against the glass. "I thought it was probably just a reflection – and it was only early evening, not night-time."

Mr Humphries nodded, as he stroked Donkey on the head. "Some people have seen things at other times too, but it's always worst after the thirteenth chime," he said in a low voice.

"Maybe it's just a faulty clock," Archie said, hopefully.

Mr Humphries shook his head. "That's what I thought too at first. When I was younger, I went to fix the clock and stop that thirteenth chime." He shivered. "That was the worst night of my life. I thought I'd never escape."

"What happened?" Lola asked. Everyone leant in.

"Between the twelfth and thirteenth chime, that's when I saw – " He closed his eyes, then snapped them open quickly, as if he didn't want to experience the memory alone. "I saw the ghost of Captain Alcott, pale as death. I heard running footsteps echoing through the clock tower, followed by terrifying screams that chilled me to the very bone. Then, as I came down the stone stairs, I saw an old woman."

"Mrs Alcott?" Lola asked.

Mr Humphries shook his head again. "This was something else. A screaming figure with hair nearly as long as the black dress she was wearing; her skin was so thin I could almost see her bones underneath. Blue veins criss-crossed her face like a map. Her eyes were dark, and they stared right at me. Her nails looked like they hadn't been cut in years."

Mr Humphries shuddered. "I've never run so fast in my life. I thought those footsteps were chasing me all the way down the tower stairs," he continued. "Then, as I was trying to get out, I felt a hand dragging me back. I fought for my life!" He paused,

his face pale at the memory.

Lola listened, wide-eyed. "What happened next?" she asked in a whisper.

"The old woman was muttering a rhyme over and over," Mr Humphries said, shaking his head.

"What was it?" Poppy asked, eagerly.

Mr Humphries shrugged. "Well, I can't remember now, but I did write it down in a notebook when I got back home. It's probably around here somewhere, but for the life of me, I've no idea where it is." He looked around the very messy room.

"How did you get away?" Archie asked, leaning forward.

Mr Humphries' eyes darted around the room before he answered. "I saw the ghost of Mrs Alcott coming towards me. But just then, the old woman with the long nails let out a piercing scream – as loud a scream as I've ever heard. She turned to Mrs Alcott and shouted, '*It's mine, it's mine*'." He shook his head. "It was like they'd forgotten all about me. I took my chance and ran. I didn't look back once until I was safe at home."

Lola and her friends sat in stunned silence as they tried to imagine this terrifying scene.

After a moment, Mr Humphries added, "But you know what was very odd? There was nothing to mend. The clock was working fine. Nothing was wrong with it." He shook his head. "I did everything I could to stop the thirteenth chime, as did my father and my grandfather before me." He looked at them all. "There have been clockmakers in the Humphries family for generations, right back to when the Alcotts were living at the hall, you see, and right up to this very day, no one has been able to discover the secret of the thirteenth chime of Alcott Hall."

Chapter 9

Later that evening, Lola, Archie and Poppy were sitting at the kitchen table at Alcott Hall, while Archie's dad and Poppy's parents chatted to Gran, Mum and Dad in the large living room.

"I hope your parents let you stay," Lola said, as she passed a plate of cookies to them.

Poppy nodded, though Lola thought she looked a bit nervous. "So do I, I mean, kind of." She gazed around. "This place is huge. There are rooms everywhere." There was a loud creak above them and Poppy jumped. "I'm beginning to wonder if it's a good idea to uncover the secrets of the thirteenth chime."

Lola was thinking the same thing, but she didn't say so. She smiled at Archie, who stared back at her from behind his glasses.

"I was thinking about what Mr Humphries said," Archie began. "There's definitely a connection between the disappearance of the Alcotts and the thirteenth chime. Remember he said that it only started after they vanished." He took another cookie while Donkey stared hopefully at the plate.

Lola nodded. "I agree." She went to the kitchen door to make sure her parents weren't coming back. "I think we need to stay up late tonight and wait for the thirteenth chime to strike."

"Do we have to?" Poppy was wide-eyed.

"If we're going to be ghost hunters, then yes, we have to," Lola added.

"I'm not sure if I want to be one right now," Poppy answered.

Even Archie, who'd been very enthusiastic up till now, looked slightly worried. "What about the mysterious old woman with the long nails? She sounds terrifying."

Poppy nodded. "Even after all this time, Mr Humphries looked frightened."

"But how are the Alcotts and the woman connected?" Lola said, thoughtfully. "I think we may be dealing with two lots of ghosts!"

Archie gasped but before he had time to say anything, Gran and Lola's parents, followed by Poppy's parents and Archie's dad, joined them.

Archie's dad smiled at him. "It turns out Lola's gran and I have met each other before. She was restoring furniture at Watley Hall, over on the other side of Cove Green, a few years ago, when I was doing the carpentry on the roof." He shook his head. "It's a small world ... Anyhow, I've agreed that you can stay here over the weekend, if you like. I'll pop over later with your pyjamas and wash bag."

Archie nodded. "Thanks, Dad. Oh, and could you bring my torch with you, please?"

Poppy's mum smiled and said, "Lola's gran said we can park our camper van in the grounds over the weekend. You can stay in the house, and we'll be nearby if you need us. The grounds stretch back over 20 acres, apparently. I think we'll set up camp on the far side of the woods."

"How about I cook something for everyone tonight?" Gran said.

Whilst the adults talked, Poppy leant in close to Lola and Archie, her eyes wide with a mix of fear and excitement. She whispered, her voice barely audible. "But what happens if we see a ghost?"

Lola felt a chill running down her spine. "Let's just hope they don't see us first."

Chapter 10

With a delicious dinner of crispy fried fish, golden plantain and rice 'n' peas long finished, Lola, Archie and Poppy sat in Lola's bedroom in the quiet of Alcott Hall. Only the sound of the summer rain could be heard pattering hard on the roof.

Lola glanced at her watch as Poppy and Archie made up their camp beds on the floor of the huge room.

"We'll need to make a plan," Lola said. "We have to make sure that we stick together and don't get split up, no matter what happens. Gran left a torch for me, so we can use that."

Archie rummaged in the bag that his dad had dropped off. "Dad said he'd put mine in my bag … Here it is." He pulled out a silver torch. "Are you scared?"

"I am," Poppy said. "I'm hoping that we don't see anything tonight."

Lola grabbed the torch from the top drawer of the old chest of drawers. "So am I, but we need to find out exactly what's going on in this place." She yawned. The sea air made her feel tired. "Why don't we set the alarm clock for quarter to midnight? Then we can have a couple of hours of sleep before we need to get up."

Poppy yawned as well. "Good idea. I could use some sleep before our midnight adventure."

Archie was already lying down on his camp bed. "Good idea."

Lola set her alarm, turned the light off, and watched the moonlight start to filter through the window, before letting her eyes close as she dropped off to sleep …

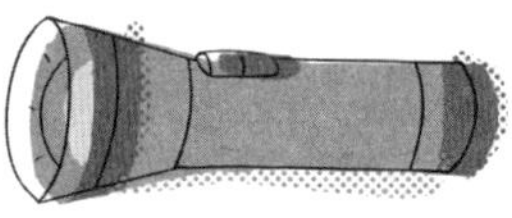

Lola woke up.

She wasn't sure how long she'd been asleep, but she felt something next to her on the bed. She moved to make way for Donkey, but as she sat up and switched on her torch, she froze. It wasn't Donkey. The little girl from the painting in the hall was there, sleeping on her bed.

Lola screamed and scrambled out of bed as the clock tower bell chimed thirteen.

Her scream woke the others, who screamed too.

"What is it?" Poppy yelled.

"The little girl from the painting downstairs – Bertha, I saw her!" Lola sobbed. "But she's gone now."

Archie leapt out of his camp bed and rushed to the light switch, but it wasn't working. Lightning struck, lighting up the room. The ghost girl hadn't gone. Now she was standing by the wardrobe. Her skin was so pale it was almost blue. Her eyes were like dark pools and staring.

"AHHHHH!" Archie yelled. They huddled together; Lola and Poppy screamed again. The little girl vanished but suddenly the walls began to bulge and ripple. Hands pressed from behind the walls, leaving visible imprints of palms and fingers moving and shifting.

"*Help us, help us.*" Whispered voices came from behind the walls and they all screamed again. They ran out of the room in fright, bumping into Lola's parents on the landing.

"What's going on? Are you all right?" Lola's dad asked.

Lola was trembling. "I think we saw a gh—"

But Archie spoke over her. "We were just telling ghost stories and frightened each other, sorry."

Lola saw him crossing his fingers.

"Well, I think it's better to stop the stories for tonight. It's very late. Now go on, get back into bed," Lola's mum said kindly. "Goodnight."

They walked back into the bedroom and Lola shone her torch around. "That was terrifying. But Mr Humphries is right – strange things happen on the thirteenth chime."

"I can't believe the alarm didn't go off," Poppy said. "What are we going to do now?"

"I think we should search the house during the day and see what we can find," Lola answered. "There are secrets hidden in these walls, and we're going to find them. We have to – before the thirteenth chime strikes again."

Chapter 11

Lola was pleased that the morning had come and they'd made it through the night after their scare. After breakfast, Lola, Poppy and Archie set about searching the house.

"Now make sure you're careful," Gran said. "Remember, there are still some rooms that haven't been touched for nearly 150 years, since the Alcotts lived here. A few of the floorboards are broken and the stairs that lead down to the servants' quarters look a bit unsteady. I don't want you hurting yourselves."

"If you need us, we'll be in the far dining room," Dad said.

"I'm sure we'll be fine," Lola answered cheerfully.

"I hope so, and this time no more ghost stories." Her mum laughed.

"We won't," Lola replied. "See you later."

They walked down the once-grand panelled corridors, which were lined with more paintings of stern-faced Alcotts, and other grim-looking people from the past. Like the portrait in Lola's room, their eyes seemed to follow them, and she shivered.

"It's so big," Poppy said. "I don't think I could find my way back to the kitchen."

Room after room was crammed with old, expensive furniture, some of it covered in white sheets. At the far end of the long corridor, they found a different kind of room.

"Wow, look at all this," Lola said. There were swords hung on the walls, glinting in the sunlight. Shelves and cabinets were filled with objects: old coins, feathers, statues and books. There was a huge walnut desk at the far end of the room.

"What is all this stuff?" Archie whispered.

Lola pulled out a book, coughing as dust flew into her face. She quickly put it back. "I don't know, maybe Captain Alcott was a collector of some sort."

While Poppy and Archie explored the room further, Lola went to the desk and opened the drawers. She rifled through them – it felt strange that she was going through someone else's belongings. "Look at all these letters," she said. "They're all handwritten in ink."

Then she picked up a leather-bound ledger and opened it. A letter slipped out and she quickly picked it up. Her eyes glanced over it.

She frowned. "Come and look at this. Don't you think this is strange?"

Poppy and Archie came to look, leaning in to see what Lola was pointing at. "It's a letter to someone called Ernest. It's only talking about how

nice the weather is and how the children are, but look, some of the letters are darker," Lola said.

Archie pushed up his glasses. "It could be an anagram. Let's see if the darker letters make a word."

They huddled together looking at the letters.

Lola read them out. "H M C I Y E N."

"I know! I know!" Poppy said, finally. "It spells CHIMNEY."

"Chimney," Lola repeated. "But why?"

Archie looked at her. "Maybe Captain Alcott hid something in one of the chimneys and he was sending a secret message to someone called Ernest?"

"You think so?" Poppy asked.

Lola shrugged. "I don't know. Maybe. It's worth a try."

Poppy glanced around. "How many chimneys do you think there are in Alcott Hall?"

"Lots!" Archie said. "Lots and lots."

"Then we might as well start looking," Lola said. "Let's see if we can find some of Captain Alcott's secrets."

Chapter 12

They began to search the house. Hour after hour, they shone the torches and poked around in every dusty, dirty fireplace in every single room, coughing and sneezing as they tried to find something. But apart from the odd bird's nest, which had tumbled down, some very large spiders and a dead rat, there was nothing to be found.

Eventually, tired and frustrated and very dirty, they ended up in the library. Like most of the rooms in Alcott Hall, it was huge, with bookshelves stretching from floor to ceiling on every wall. Cobwebs glistened in the beams of sunlight streaming through the tall windows and a thick layer of dust sat on every book.

"What are we going to do now?" Archie said, wiping dirt off his glasses.

"Maybe we missed something," Lola answered. She ran her finger along the spines of the leather books.

"But we've checked all the fireplaces we could, apart from the one in the living room where your gran and parents are working," Poppy said, sounding disappointed.

"I don't know," Lola sighed. She absentmindedly pulled books off the shelves, flipped through pages, and put them back. She wasn't sure what they were supposed to do next.

"Hey, that's weird," Archie exclaimed.

Archie was pointing to the gap left by the book Lola had just pulled out. Instead of seeing the back of the bookshelf, there was something else.

"Help me get these other books out," Archie said quickly.

They carefully removed the surrounding books, revealing more of what was hidden behind … It was a door – a secret door disguised as a bookshelf.

"Should we try to open it?" Archie whispered.

Lola nodded. She spotted a small metal latch at the side of the bookshelf. When she pulled it, the shelf swung away from the wall, showing the door behind it. They gently pushed, but it didn't budge.

"Look," Poppy said, pointing. The door was locked shut.

Lola examined the lock closely. It was an old-fashioned padlock, but instead of numbers, it had letters. There were seven dials, each with letters on it.

"It's like the padlock on Dad's shed," Lola explained, "but with letters instead of numbers, and more wheel dials."

Archie rattled it. "How are we supposed to guess the right word? It could be anything!"

Poppy's eyes suddenly widened. "Wait! The word we worked out – *chimney*."

Lola nodded excitedly. "And there are seven letters in *chimney* – exactly the same as the number of dials!"

With shaking hands, Poppy turned the dials: C-H-I-M-N-E-Y. They all held their breath as she pulled on the lock. For a moment, nothing happened. Then, with a click, the lock sprang open.

Lola exchanged a glance with Poppy and Archie. What was behind this hidden door?

Chapter 13

The door creaked open, releasing a blast of cold, damp air that smelt strongly of the sea. Lola glanced at the others and asked nervously, "What do you think? Shall we?"

Archie and Poppy nodded.

"Wait," Archie said. He rushed over to a small desk, pulled it over and put it in front of the door. "I don't want it to close and trap us down there."

Poppy pulled a face. "Good idea. I definitely don't want to be locked down there." She gazed into the darkness.

"Oh no," Archie sighed. "My torch has run out of batteries."

So Lola switched on her torch and led the

way down some spiral stone stairs. The torch beam showed worn steps and, as they descended further, the stairs narrowed, and the smooth walls gave way to rough, jagged rock. The air grew colder and heavier with the scent of salt.

"Are you all right?" Lola whispered over her shoulder.

"I think so," Poppy said, sounding far from all right.

"What about you, Archie?"

"Yeah, I'm good," he said. But there was a wobble of fear in his voice. "I wish my torch was still working."

They reached the bottom of the stairs and walked along a twisting rocky tunnel. Lola could hear their footsteps echoing around. Water dripped somewhere in the darkness of the tunnel; each drop sounding like a whispering voice.

"This tunnel is built into the cliff," Archie said. "My dad told me there are secret smugglers' tunnels all along the coast."

Suddenly, the tunnel opened into a vast cove. "Wow!" Lola said, as she watched the sea crash against the rocky walls. Through the cove's mouth there was nothing but ocean, which now looked dark under the gathering storm clouds.

"Let's see what's in here." Lola's torch beam moved along the wet rocks, casting long, moving shadows. In the far corner, she spotted something. She let out a piercing scream, causing Poppy and Archie to do the same.

There was an old wooden chest, and next to it was a life-sized antique porcelain doll with cracked features and eyes that seemed to stare back, flashing in the darkness.

"That's so spooky," Lola said, trembling.

They walked towards the wooden chest, making sure that they didn't slip on the slimy algae-covered rocks.

"I don't know if I want to do this," Lola

said quietly, as she stared at the chest.

"I don't either," Archie agreed.

"I'll do it then." Poppy's hands were shaking as she slowly opened the chest. "Wow," she said, slowly.

Inside the chest were gold coins, jewels, silver cups, and beautiful necklaces and bracelets.

"Do you think this belonged to Captain Alcott?" Lola said.

"Probably. Maybe this cove was like his safe," Archie said.

Lola nodded. "We did find the combination code to the lock in one of his letters, so that makes sense."

Just then, a whisper echoed through the cove, seeming to come from everywhere and nowhere. Then it became louder. "*Help us ... free us ...*" voices pleaded, and a shadow passed across the entrance.

The sea darkened, waves crashed violently, and as the foam sprayed high into the air, Lola gasped. In the froth, she was sure she saw a person's face forming and vanishing.

"Did you see that?" she whispered, pointing with a shaking hand.

Archie and Poppy nodded, their eyes wide with terror.

The doll's fingers twitched, scraping against the chest's metal clasp. Then a cold wind whipped through the cove, carrying more whispers, growing louder. The torch flickered, and they were plunged into darkness. When the torch light returned, the doll was no longer there.

"Run!" Lola yelled. They turned and raced back through the tunnel, the sound of chasing footsteps echoed around the walls, and the whispers followed them.

Gasping for breath, they finally reached the library. They pushed the desk out of the way and slammed the secret door, sliding the bolt shut. Archie fumbled with the combination lock.

"Quick, hurry up!" Lola said, urgently.

"I'm trying." Archie sounded panicked.

Finally, they managed to shut the door, and they leant against it. Lola could feel her heart pounding. Suddenly, loud banging echoed from the other side of the door, making them jump and scream once again.

Trembling, Lola glanced at Poppy and Archie. "I don't think the thirteenth chime has finished with us yet."

Chapter 14

It was late afternoon and Lola, Archie and Poppy huddled at the kitchen table speaking in whispers, still shaken by what they'd discovered at Alcott Hall. They'd washed off the grime from exploring the cove and changed their clothes, but they couldn't stop thinking about the clues they'd found. When Poppy's mum appeared with a chocolate cake from the bakery, they welcomed the distraction, but their minds kept drifting back to the mystery that seemed to grow bigger.

Lola's gran and parents sat outside on the stone patio chatting to Archie's dad, who'd popped in to check everything was all right, but Lola still kept her voice down. "So why do you think Captain Alcott hid a chest of treasure in the secret cove?" Lola asked, frowning.

Poppy shrugged. "I don't know. But what really scares me are those voices we heard. Who do they belong to? And why were they asking for help?"

Archie gazed at Lola and Poppy. "How can we help them when we don't know who they are?"

"All these things must be connected, but I just don't know how yet." Lola was determined to get to the bottom of the mystery. "Maybe if we find out why the thirteenth chime started when the Alcotts vanished, we might be able to solve everything else. Hopefully Mum, Dad and Gran will go to bed early tonight, then this time we can stay up and see what happens," Lola whispered.

Archie paled. "I hope we don't see that child again. She gave me the creeps."

"Me too," Poppy said, wiping sticky chocolate cake from her mouth.

"*Hello!*" came a voice from the garden.

Lola, Archie and Poppy looked over and waved when they saw Mr Humphries talking to Lola's parents.

"Hello, Mr Humphries," Lola called out.

Archie and Poppy smiled.

Mr Humphries shuffled into the kitchen towards them.

"What are you doing here?" Lola asked, remembering that Mr Humphries had said he'd never come to Alcott Hall again.

"I'm glad I've caught you all," Mr Humphries said, settling into a chair. "It was you I've come to see."

"Would you like a cup of tea and cake?" Lola asked.

"That would be lovely," Mr Humphries said.

She got up and poured him a cup of tea from the pot and cut him the biggest slice of chocolate cake.

Mr Humphries smiled. His eyes twinkled kindly as he looked at her from underneath his bushy eyebrows. "That rhyme I was talking about, the one the old woman was chanting. Do you remember I said I'd written it down?" he said.

Poppy nodded.

"Well, I found it." Mr Humphries patted his pocket.

"You did?" Archie said, excitedly.

Mr Humphries nodded. "I knew I'd put it somewhere safely. Mind, it was over 60 years ago," he chuckled. "But then my wife reminded me that I often keep important things in biscuit tins, and what do you know, it was hidden inside an old grandfather clock in a biscuit tin. I hadn't looked at it since I put it in there over half a century ago."

Lola tried not to be impatient as Mr Humphries slowly reached into his pocket and pulled out a crumpled piece of paper with a large jam stain on it.

"I'll read it to you, shall I?" he said.

"Yes, please," Lola smiled at him.

Mr Humphries cleared his throat, before reading what was on the paper.

"Until the hour of midnight I did wait,

I warned you not to be too late.

Return the Crimson Heart by night,

To the emperor's pool in pale moonlight.

My words ignored, now face your fate,

The bell has struck, so accept your state:

The midnight clock rang out its time,

You're trapped forever in the Thirteenth Chime."

Mr Humphries looked at them and for a moment no one said anything.

"What do you think it means?" Archie said.

"I don't know," Mr Humpries admitted. "But she said the rhyme over and over again. It was hard to forget it."

"So, the old woman wanted something returned by midnight?" Lola said.

Mr Humphries nodded. "That's what it looks like but whoever was supposed to return the item, *didn't*."

"That's why it says, *my words ignored, now face your fate,*" Poppy said. "They didn't do what they were told."

Mr Humphries looked at them. "It sounds like some sort of curse to me."

"A curse!" Lola covered her mouth. She was thinking about the voices, calling for help in the cove.

Mr Humphries nodded.

"What's the *crimson heart*?" Archie said, puzzled.

"I've no idea, Archie," Mr Humphries said. "I remember it puzzled me at the time."

Lola sighed. "So, all we know is that someone had to do something by midnight, and they didn't."

"But what does she mean by *the emperor's pool*?" Poppy asked.

At that moment, Archie's dad walked in. "I was coming to check on you, Archie, but I see Mr Humphries is keeping you busy. The emperor's pool, did I hear you say?"

Archie glanced at Lola. She hoped Archie's dad hadn't overheard anything else.

"I haven't heard it called that for a long time," he said. "When I was young, I spent many happy hours there swimming in it or sunbathing on the rocks around it."

Archie sat up. "Where is it?"

"It's the large rock pool at the end of the pebble beach under the steep cliff," Archie's dad said. "That's what they used to call it for some reason, but over time the name got lost." He smiled at Mr Humphries. "I'll give you a lift back to the village, if you like."

Lola had a sudden thought. "Oh, Mr Humphries, before you go … you don't know anyone called Ernest, do you? Someone the Alcotts might have known?"

Mr Humphries thought for a minute. "Ernest? Hmm. I believe there was a nephew called Ernest – in the United States." Then he shuffled off. "Cheerio now."

"So that's who the letter and the secret code was for," Archie said.

Lola nodded. "But Captain Alcott must have disappeared before he could send the letter."

"Now what do we do?" Poppy asked.

Lola lowered her voice. "We go to the emperor's pool tonight … on the thirteenth chime."

Chapter 15

That night, Lola, Archie and Poppy made their way down the thin path to the beach. It was pitch black and it had been raining again, so the path was slippery, making them walk slower than they wanted to.

"Be careful!" Lola shouted, as she shone the torch in front of her.

The wind howled around them, whipping up their hair and clothes. Above, dark storm clouds raced across the night sky.

As cautious as Lola was, she found herself stumbling and slipping as she continued towards the far side of the beach. They needed to hurry but she didn't want to fall.

Archie pressed his watch which had a light on

it. “I hope we get there in time,” he shouted back. They could hardly hear each other over the wind and the roar of the sea.

“We’re nearly there,” Lola said, wishing she’d put on a warmer jumper. Even though it was summer, the night-time storms were cold and sharp. In the distance, they heard the chime of the bell on the clock tower starting to strike. They were too late!

They quickened their pace, but just as their feet

hit the pebbles on the beach, Lola heard it – the deep toll of the thirteenth chime.

"No! We've missed it," Poppy said. "What should we do? Should we go back?"

Lola gazed around. The moon had come out from behind the clouds, streaming light down onto the sea, which was a churning angry mass of black water and massive waves, slamming against the shore.

Lightning flashed, illuminating the beach and Lola stepped closer to Archie. She tried not to scream as she saw an old woman emerging from the sea.

"Quick!" Archie hissed, pulling them behind a large, jagged rock where they could hide in the shadows. They crouched down, peering out at the terrifying sight.

Lola gasped. She was like no woman Lola had ever seen before. She wore a long, black dress trailing behind her and her nails were long and sharp, scraping against the rocks with a sound that set Lola's teeth on edge.

Poppy's eyes widened in horror. "I think that's the old woman Mr Humphries described," she whispered.

Lola continued to watch, noticing how the woman's hair was a tangled mess of dark seaweed, dripping and moving as if it were alive. In the flashes of lightning, she could see things moving in it – tiny crabs and fish, struggling to free themselves. Her face was long and thin, stretched over sharp bones, with skin that was almost see-through, and a scaly sheen that caught in the moonlight.

As she dragged her feet along the stones, Lola noticed her toenails were as long as those on her hands and each step she took left deep scrapes in the wet sand.

Suddenly, the woman started screaming and muttering, her voice rasping and gurgling.

Lola huddled closer to Archie and Poppy behind the rock.

"Listen," Archie hissed, gripping Lola's arm tightly. "Listen to what she's saying … It's the rhyme. The one Mr Humphries told us!"

Lola strained to hear the words; the woman's voice was rising and falling above the sound of the waves.

"Where's she going?" Poppy asked, as the woman began to walk towards one of the coves.

"I don't know, but maybe we should follow her," Lola said, her voice shaking.

"Follow her … do we have to?" Poppy looked terrified.

"We need to make sure she doesn't see us, but at least we'll know where she's going," Lola said.

Just as they were about to creep towards her, a familiar bark split the air. Donkey came bounding down the path towards them, his tail wagging.

"Donkey!" Lola said. "How did he get here?"

"We must have left the back door open," Archie said.

The moment Donkey reached them, the woman vanished, leaving nothing but the echo of her chilling voice and deep scrapes in the sand.

Chapter 16

The attic of Alcott Manor was a maze of dusty boxes and forgotten memories. Lola, Archie and Poppy had volunteered to help Gran move the boxes so she could get to some of the furniture she needed to restore. Sunlight streamed through the small windows of the attic roof.

Lola yawned. She was so tired from last night's adventures.

"Careful with that one, Lola," Gran called out, as Lola struggled with a heavy box. But it was too late – the box slipped from her grasp, hitting the floor with a dull thud. Its contents spilt across the worn wooden boards.

"Oh no! I'm so sorry, Gran!" Lola said, as she knelt to gather the scattered items that had fallen out of the box. Picking them up, she realised it was a stack of old newspapers. "Wow, look at these. They're so old … Look at the date; they're from 1873." She looked at some more. "This one's from July 1874 … and these are from 1875."

Archie and Poppy came over to help her.

"That's the year that the Alcotts vanished," Archie said quietly so Gran wouldn't hear. He gently picked one up, careful not to tear the fragile paper. "They're so old!"

Poppy opened one of the newspapers, her eyes wide. "Look at these illustrations!"

"I guess they didn't have photographs in papers in those days, so they had to draw pictures instead," Lola said, remembering one of her History lessons.

Poppy carefully continued to turn the pages, reading the stories and news and looking at the advertisements for penny-farthing bicycles and corsets.

As Poppy turned another page, something caught Lola's eye. "Hey, wait a minute. Look at that." She pointed to an article. "*Local Hero Returns with Treasure. Captain Alfred Alcott, an esteemed explorer and collector, has once again astounded locals with his latest discovery.*"

Lola looked at them, then glanced back down at the article. "*Captain Alcott recovered a chest containing priceless objects from the* Crimson Heart, *a ship that sank 100 years ago with its crew and its owner, Count Robinson and his wife, Countess Robinson.*"

"Crimson heart! That's part of the rhyme,"

Archie said quickly.

Poppy nodded. "So, as this paper is dated 1875, the ship must have sunk in 1775. Wow."

Lola glanced down and began to read again. "*The chest was at the very depths of Davy's Locker itself.*"

"What's Davy's Locker?" Archie asked.

"I don't know … Gran," Lola called over to Gran, who was busy admiring one of the old wooden chairs she was going to restore. "Gran, do you know what Davy's Locker is?"

"It's an old sailor's sea term. It means the bottom of the ocean – where sunken ships and drowned sailors are said to rest," Gran told them.

A chill ran down Lola's spine.

Poppy started to read the rest. "*Among the items, Captain Alcott said he recovered a ruby necklace of extraordinary size and beauty. He named it the Crimson Heart after the sunken ship.*"

"But why was he able to keep it?" Lola said.

"If someone finds an old shipwreck that nobody owns any more, they get to keep everything they find inside it," Archie said. "I remember Dad telling me that when some people found another old shipwreck off the coast last year while they were fishing. Not that there was anything in that apart from old metal plates and mugs."

Lola gasped. Poppy and Archie's eyes widened as they looked at what she was pointing at in the newspaper. It was an illustration of a large, teardrop-shaped stone hanging from a necklace next to the article about Captain Alcott.

"That must be the Crimson Heart necklace," Poppy said.

Suddenly, Lola stood up. "I've seen it before. Come on, I'll show you."

They raced down the attic stairs. Lola held onto the old newspaper whilst Archie and Poppy exchanged puzzled glances.

Lola skidded to a halt in front of the large portrait of the Alcott family in the main hallway. "Look!" She held up the newspaper illustration next to the painting. "It's the same necklace! Mrs Alcott is wearing the Crimson Heart."

"But what does it mean?" Poppy asked.

Lola's mind was racing. "Remember the old woman we saw on the beach?" The others nodded, shuddering at the memory. "What if ... what if she's the ghost of the ruby's rightful owner? What if that was Countess Robinson, who drowned at sea when the boat sank?"

"And Captain Alcott found the ruby and brought it back, not knowing what would happen," Archie added, catching on.

"So, the ghost of Countess Robinson obviously wants the ruby, but if she's still roaming the beach, it looks like Captain Alcott didn't give it back to her," Lola said.

"Why would he?" Poppy said. "If she just turned up on the doorstep, he probably didn't know who she was, *and* she looks terrifying. When the countess didn't get the ruby, she must have put a curse on the family."

They were silent for a moment and Lola thought about what Mr Humphries had said. Then she thought about the rhyme. "That's why they're all trapped in the thirteenth chime. She cursed them and they were somehow trapped between two worlds. That's why no one ever found them," she said softly. Then she glanced around. "But their spirits are unable to rest. That's why Alcott Hall's haunted. They've been waiting all this time for someone to help them find their way home, to finally be at peace."

"They've obviously been trying to escape, but they can't because they're stuck in time forever, because they didn't give the necklace back to Countess Robinson by midnight," Poppy added, understanding. "Like the rhyme says:

My words ignored, now face your fate,

The bell has struck, so accept your state:

The midnight clock rang out its time,

You're trapped forever in the Thirteenth Chime."

"*We* could give the Crimson Heart back," Lola said suddenly.

Archie and Poppy stared at Lola.

"The Alcotts need our help," Lola whispered. "All of them: Captain Alcott, Mrs Alcott, their children."

Archie didn't say anything for a moment but then he nodded. "Lola's right, we need to free them so they can rest in peace."

"OK, let's give the Crimson Heart back to its rightful owner," Poppy smiled, nervously.

"I think I know where the necklace might be," Lola said. "Then at the thirteenth chime, we'll wait at the emperor's pool and give the necklace back to her, and then the curse might be lifted."

"Do you think we'll be safe?" Poppy asked.

Lola glanced at her. "I hope so … I really, really hope so."

Chapter 17

It was almost midnight. Down in the cove, under the beam of torchlight, Lola's hands trembled as she searched through the old chest. Archie had placed the spooky antique doll to the far side of the cove which Lola was grateful for. She moved the gold coins to the side, and the diamond bracelets and silver cups.

"Maybe Captain Alcott left the chest here for safekeeping, after the ghost of the countess showed up asking for the return of the Crimson Heart," Archie whispered.

Lola glanced up at him. "Maybe. I guess we'll never know for sure."

Lola continued to look through the chest as Poppy held the torch for her. Suddenly, her fingers brushed against something cold and smooth, and she gently pulled it out, breathless, as the beautiful ruby necklace caught the light. She held it up to show the others. "The Crimson Heart."

"It's gorgeous," Poppy said.

A distant rumble of thunder sounded, and the wind whirled around them. "We need to hurry," Lola said, clutching the necklace tightly in her hand.

"What about the rest of the treasure?" Archie asked.

Lola glanced at the chest. "Let's just leave it here. It's safe where it is. This is where it belongs."

They dashed out of the cove and back up the stairs through the secret door hidden behind the bookshelf. Then they ran out of Alcott Hall, along the top of the cliff and to the steep path which would lead them onto the beach which stretched before them.

"I'll lead the way," Archie said, and he ran in front with the torch. Lola and Poppy followed him; the roar of the waves grew louder.

They hurried over the pebbly beach and across some rocks, careful not to slip.

"It's just over there!" Archie shouted.

Ahead, Lola could see the emperor's pool in the moonlight – a massive rock formation carved by centuries of tides. "How long have we got?" she asked.

Archie glanced at his watch. "About five minutes. Come on."

They ran faster. Panting heavily, they got to the pool and stood near the edge as the waves crashed against nearby rocks, sending spray high into the air.

"Now what?" Poppy asked.

Before Lola could answer, a deep sound cut through the storm – the clock tower bell. They stood closely together, counting the chimes.

"One ... two ... three ..."

Lola's heart raced as she continued to count.

"Ten ... eleven ... twelve ..."

She held her breath, waiting. For a moment, there was nothing but the sound of the wind and waves. Then, the thirteenth chime rang out, deeper and more threatening than the others. As the sound rang, Lola turned towards the sea as a ghostly shriek split the air.

She stepped back as she saw the old woman emerge once again from the churning sea, more terrifying than the last time. Her hair writhed, tangled with shells and bones. Her skin glistened with scales, and Lola saw with horror that her eyelids were transparent, revealing eyes like those of a dead fish.

The woman screamed and screeched, chanting the same rhyme over and over again.

"Return the Crimson Heart by night,

To the emperor's pool in pale moonlight."

The old woman was getting closer, and Lola could feel Poppy shaking. Then suddenly, Lola shouted. "I have the Crimson Heart! I have the Crimson Heart! I have what you want."

The old woman froze; her fishy eyes fixed on Lola.

Lola swallowed hard and took a step forward, holding out the necklace. "Look it's here. It's here." Lola shook as she held out her hand towards the terrifying figure.

The old woman's eyes moved to the necklace, and she reached out, her long nails scraping Lola's palm as she scooped the necklace up. Lola bit back a cry, feeling the sting of the old woman's scratch.

For a moment nothing happened. The old woman just continued to stare at Lola, who was shaking in fear. Then without warning, she cackled so loudly it hurt Lola's ears, and a huge wave rose up behind her. Clasping the necklace, the old woman opened her arms and let the wave crash over her, swallowing her up in a whirl of foam and fury.

And then there was silence.

The storm faded away. The sea was calm, and the wind was now only a gentle breeze.

"Is ... is that it?" Poppy whispered. "Is it over? Is the curse over? Is it broken?"

Lola looked at her. "I don't know. Come on." She turned and started to run back towards Alcott Hall, with the others following her.

As they burst through the front door, and into the hallway, they skidded to a stop. There, in front of the fireplace, stood the Alcott family. Captain Alcott, tall and proud in his navy suit. His wife, elegant in her Victorian gown. Their children, next to them. They all turned to face Lola, Archie and Poppy, smiles breaking across their faces.

The Alcotts' lips moved. Although no sound came out, Lola could see they were saying,

“*Thank you.*”

“You’re welcome,” Lola whispered.

They nodded, and right then, the Alcotts began to fade, turning into a misty silvery smoke, flowing into the painting above the fireplace.

Lola stared at the painting, stunned. “Look! Look at that!”

The painting had changed. The family was still there, but now they were smiling, their faces full of joy and peace. And Mrs Alcott’s neck was bare – the Crimson Heart was gone.

“I think the curse of the thirteenth chime has been lifted. It’s finally been lifted. The Alcotts are finally at peace,” Lola said softly, and smiled at her friends.

From that day onwards, no one heard the thirteenth chime of Alcott Hall ever again.

Book talk questions

Which of the characters did you relate to the most?

What do you think happened to the Alcott family after they were released?

Did you find any parts of the book scary?

What do you think you would have done in Lola's position, after hearing the story of Alcott Hall?

Do you think Countess Robinson was right to curse the Alcotts?

Have you ever had an unexpected holiday like Lola's?

Do you think it's right that you can keep things from shipwrecks?

Who was your favourite character in the book?

Do you think you've ever seen a ghost?

Do you know any other ghost stories?

Ask the author

How did you first get into writing?

When I was a child I began to write stories for myself as I couldn't find the stories I enjoyed so I started writing the stories I wanted to read!

J. P. Rose

What was your inspiration for *The Thirteenth Chime of Alcott Hall*?

I love the Victorian ages and the idea of a family going missing one night seemed an exciting basis of a story within an old gothic mansion on a windswept cliff, and the idea that a clock strikes 13 times, but no one knows why sent chills down my spine. But the name Alcott Hall was inspired by the author who wrote *Little Women*. Her name was Louisa May Alcott.

Have you ever had a ghostly experience?

I'm not sure if I have had any true ghostly experiences, but my imagination makes me think I have. Also when I was a child my sister and I used to love telling each other ghost stories and seeing if we could frighten each other, so I was convinced that a ghost lived down the plug hole!

Who is your favourite character in the book?
Apart from Donkey? I have to say I don't have a favourite as they were so much fun to write, but I do love the friendship between the children.

Which was your favourite part of the book to write?
When they saw the ghosts!

What's your favourite thing about being an author?
You get to go on lots of adventures and journeys in your head, and it's also wonderful to meet and hear from young readers.

How did you come up with the setting for the book?
I love rugged coastlines, not only for their beauty but for their spookiness, so I thought it was the perfect setting.

What do you most want readers to take away from reading this book?
I want them to start falling in love with spooky stories!

Collins BIG CAT

Published by Collins
An imprint of HarperCollins*Publishers*

The News Building
1 London Bridge Street
London SE1 9GF
UK

Macken House
39/40 Mayor Street Upper
Dublin 1
D01 C9W8
Ireland

Text © J. P. Rose 2025
Design and illustrations © HarperCollins*Publishers* Limited 2025

10 9 8 7 6 5 4 3 2 1

ISBN 978-0-00-874481-6

All rights reserved. No part of this publication may be reproduced, stored in a retrieval system, or transmitted in any form by any means, electronic, mechanical, photocopying, recording or otherwise, without the prior written permission of the Publisher or a licence permitting restricted copying in the United Kingdom issued by the Copyright Licensing Agency Ltd, 5th Floor, Shackleton House, 4 Battle Bridge Lane, London SE1 2HX.

Without limiting the author's and publisher's exclusive rights, any unauthorised use of this publication to train generative artificial intelligence (AI) technologies is expressly prohibited. HarperCollins also exercise their rights under Article 4(3) of the Digital Single Market Directive 2019/790 and expressly reserve this publication from the text and data mining exception.

British Library Cataloguing-in-Publication Data
A catalogue record for this publication is available from the British Library.

Author: J. P. Rose
Illustrator: Monique Steel (Illo Agency)
Publisher: Laura White
Commissioning editor: Holly Woolnough
Development editor: Zoë Clarke
Product manager: Holly Woolnough
Content editor: Selin Akca
Copyeditor: Sally Byford
Proofreader: Catherine Dakin
Reviewer: Lisa Davis
Cover designer: Sarah Finan
Internal design: 2Hoots Publishing Services Ltd
Typesetter: Jouve India Ltd
Production controller: Katharine Willard

Collins would like to thank the teachers and children at Grange Primary School, Southwark, for being part of the development of Big Cat Read On.

Printed in the UK.

MIX
Paper | Supporting responsible forestry
FSC™ C007454
FSC www.fsc.org

This book contains FSC™ certified paper and other controlled sources to ensure responsible forest management.

For more information visit: www.harpercollins.co.uk/green

Made with responsibly sourced paper and vegetable ink

Scan to see how we are reducing our environmental impact.

Get the latest Collins Big Cat news at
collins.co.uk/collinsbigcat

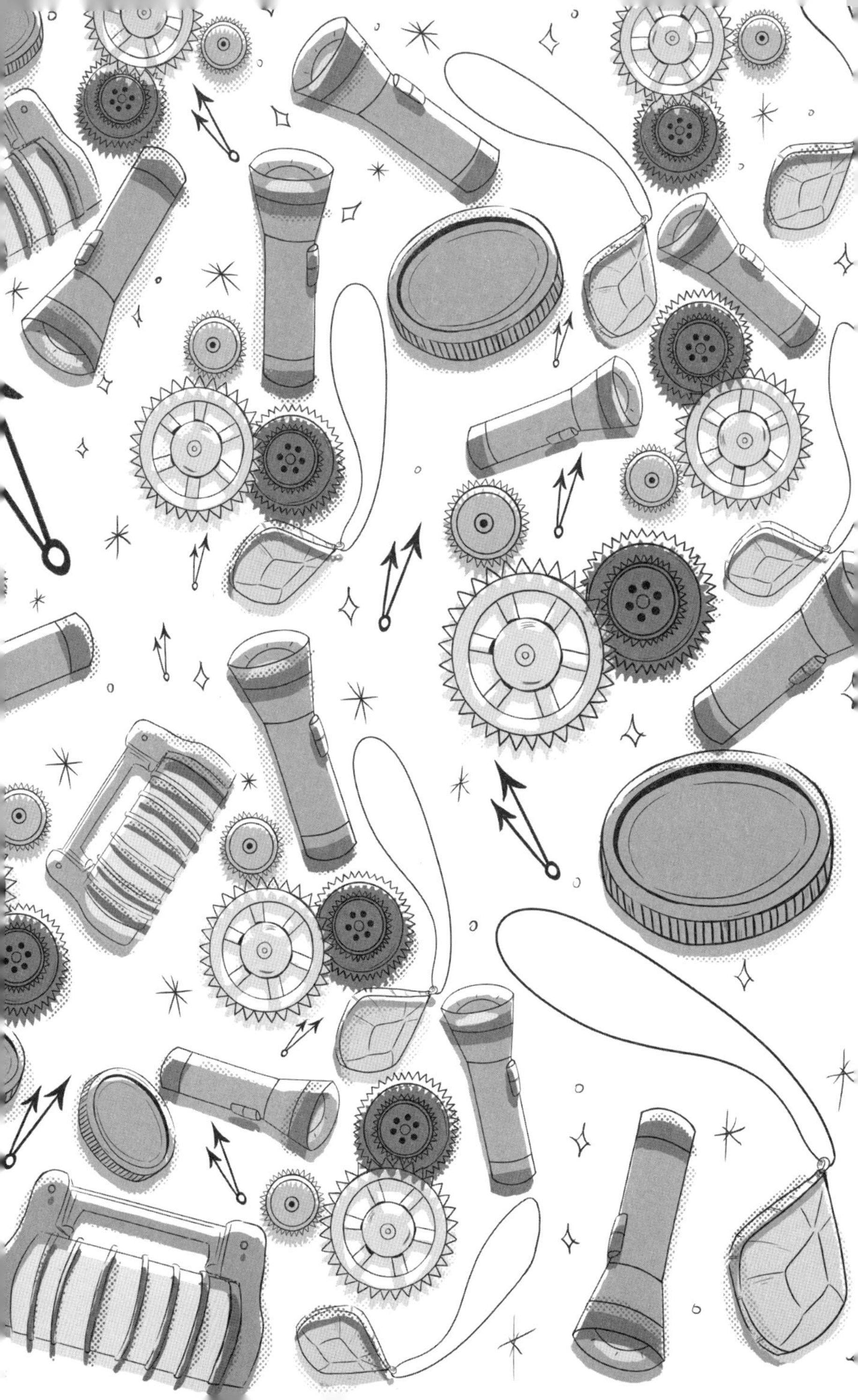

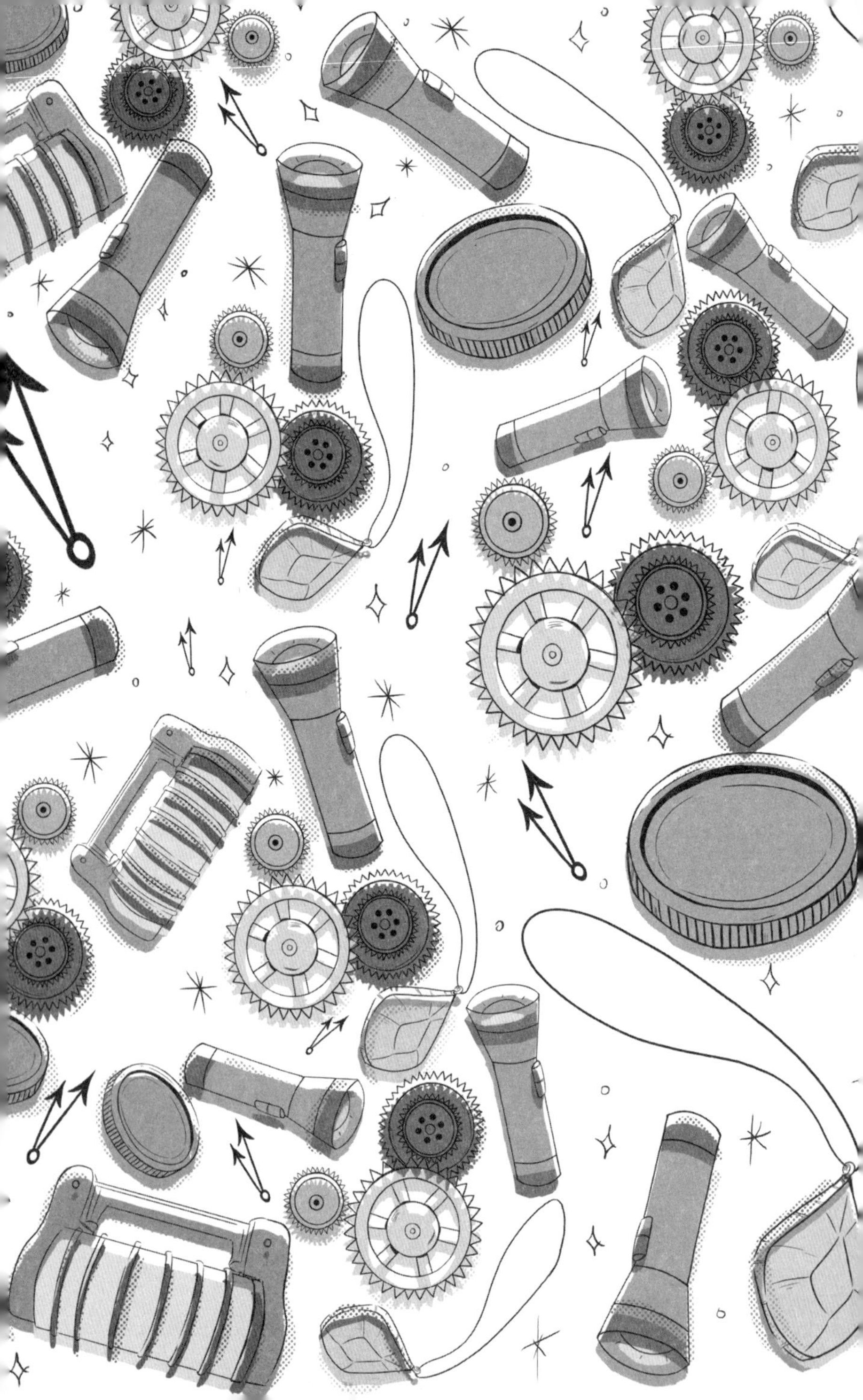